PALM BEACH COUNTY

W9-ARA-130   4198

ANGELA'S AIRPLANE

A Note from
Robert Munsch

A long, long, LONG time ago when I was in first grade, my class had 60 kids in it!

The teacher didn't read any books and neither did the kids. It was not fun.

Well, here is a book that is fun to read for both you and your grown-ups.

READERS RULE!

High-Frequency Words

Practice reading these high-frequency words in the story:

anyone   find   once   they

Meet the Characters

Get to know the characters from the story by looking at the pictures and names below:

Angela

Angela's father

Voice on the radio

Self-Talk

In this story, Angela talks to herself to encourage herself to act bravely. If you were going to encourage yourself to be brave and take a risk, what would you say? (e.g., "I got this!", "I'm just going to try," "My brain learns when I make a mistake"). Once you decide on a line, practice saying this line when something is tough and see if it helps you take more risks or feel more confident!

Pretend to Fly a Plane

One of the most exciting parts of the story is when Angela has to fly the airplane. Read the instructions that the voice on the radio gives Angela, and pretend to fly the airplane just like her!

"Turn the steering wheel to the left."

"Now pull back on the wheel."

Do you think flying a plane would be this easy? What actions would you add if you had to fly the plane?

Phonics

There is an **A** sound at the beginning of the word **Angela**.

Can you make an **A** sound?

Pay close attention to the shape of your mouth as you make the sound. It might be helpful to make this sound while you look in a mirror to see the shape your mouth makes.

Try these different activities to help practice the letter **A** sound.

1. Take a close look around you and try to find three objects that start with the same sound.

2. Think of three other words that also start with the same sound. As an extra challenge, can you think of any words that end with an **A** sound?

3. A simple word that has the **A** sound at the beginning is the word **ant**. As you read this word, pay attention to the two other letter sounds in the word.

4. When two words rhyme, they have the same sounds at the end of the word. Take a look at the pictures below and point to any of the words that rhyme with **ant.**

plant   **pant**   **apple**

5. While you read, look out for other **A** sounds at the beginning of a word throughout the story. You can see the sound easily because it will be written in a different color.

ANGELA'S AIRPLANE

Story by **Robert Munsch**
Art by **Michael Martchenko**

**annick
press**
toronto · berkeley

To Billy, Sheila, and
Kathleen Cronin

When Angela's father

took her to the airport,

a terrible thing happened:

Angela's father got lost.

Angela looked under airplanes, on top of airplanes, and beside airplanes, but she couldn't find him anywhere.

She looked inside an airplane.

Her father wasn't there, and neither was anyone else.

Angela sat down in a seat that had

lots of buttons all around it.

She said to herself, "Don't you think

it's okay if I push just one button?

Oh yes, it's okay."

Then she pressed the bright red button

and right away, the door closed.

Angela said, "Don't you think it's okay if I push just one more button? Oh yes, it's okay."

She pushed the yellow button, and right away, the lights came on. Then she pushed the green button, and right away, the motor came on: VROOM, VROOM.

Angela said, "Yikes," and pushed all the buttons at once. The airplane went right up into the air.

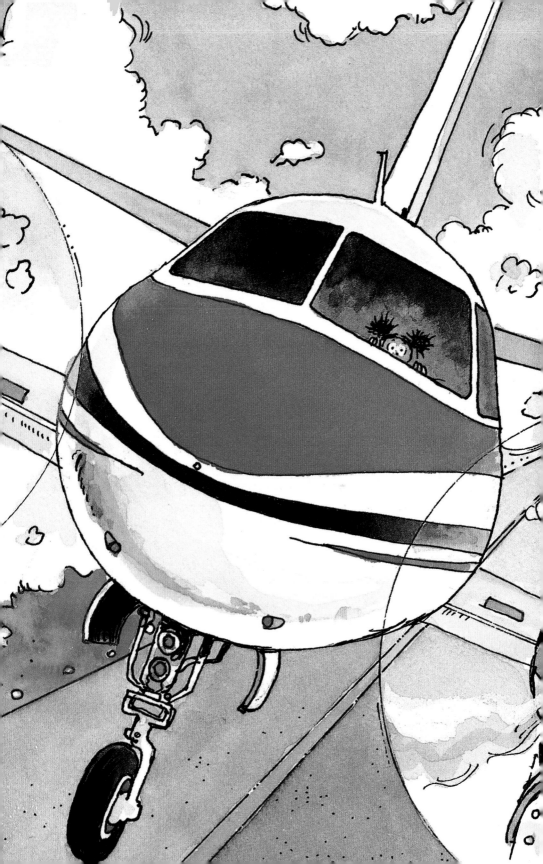

Angela saw that she was very high in the sky. She didn't know how to get down.

The only thing to do was to push one more button, so she pushed the black button. It was the radio button.

A voice said, "Bring back that airplane, you thief, you."

Angela said, "My name is Angela. I am five years old and I don't know how to fly airplanes."

"Oh dear," said the voice. "What a mess. Listen carefully, Angela. Turn the steering wheel to the left."

Angela turned the wheel.

The airplane went in a big circle and came back to the airport.

"Now pull back on the wheel," said the voice.

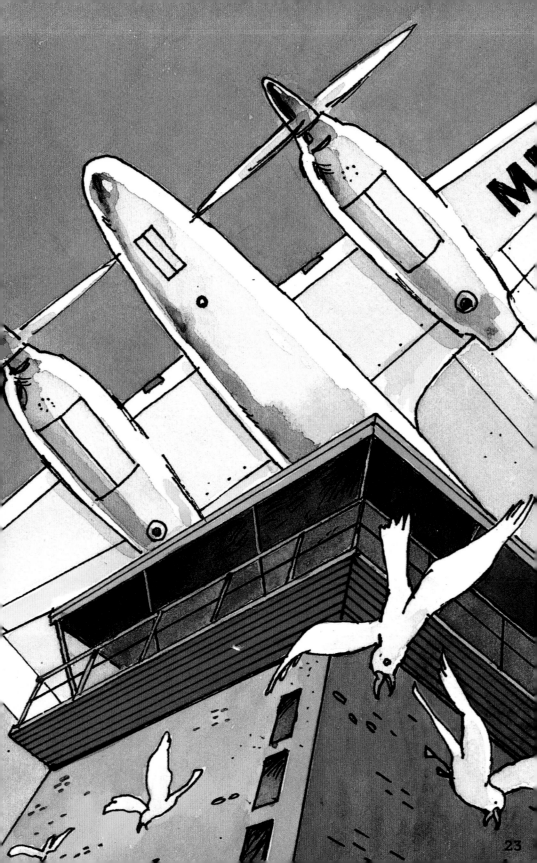

23

Angela pulled back on the wheel.

The airplane slowly went down to the runway.

It bounced once; it bounced twice.

One wing scraped the ground.

The whole plane smashed and broke into little pieces.

Angela didn't even have a scratch.

25

Police cars, ambulances, and fire
trucks sped out of the terminal.
All sorts of people came running.
In front of everybody was Angela's
father.

"Are you all right?" asked her father.

"Yes," said Angela.

"Promise me you will never fly
another airplane," said her father.

"I promise, I promise, I promise,"
said Angela very loudly.

Angela didn't fly an airplane

for a very long time.

But when she grew up,

she didn't become a doctor,

or a truck driver, or a nurse.

She became an airplane pilot.

Retell Activity

Look closely at each picture and describe what is happening in your own words giving as much detail as possible.

When I Grow Up...

At the end of the story, we find out that Angela becomes a pilot when she grows up!

What do you want to be when you grow up? Think of something that you would have to do now to prepare for your future job as an adult.

Take a look at the pictures below and brainstorm different jobs these children might do when they grow up if they love these activities:

Spot the Differences

Look carefully at the two pictures below.
Point to all the differences you can find.

1. Angela's shirt color   2. Missing dials   3. Angela's hand
4. Missing switches   5. Missing seatbelt

Getting Ready for Reading Tips

- Pick a time during the day when you are most excited to read. This could be when you wake up, after a meal, or right before bedtime.

- Create a special space in your home for reading with some blankets and pillows. The inside of a closet, under a table, or under a bed can make the perfect cozy spot.

- Before you start reading, do a quick look at all the pictures and suggest what the story might be about.

- Can you find the part of the story that repeats?

- Can you add actions like claps, stomps, or jumps to match what is being said to make the words come alive?

- Try to use silly voices for the different characters in the story. Think about changing the volume (e.g., loud, soft), the speed you use to say the words (e.g., fast, super slowly), and how you say the words (e.g., like an animal, like a superhero, like someone older or younger).

- What makes this story silly or funny?

- What part(s) of the story would never happen in real life?

Collect them all!

Adapted from the originals for beginner readers and packed with **Classic Munsch** fun!

Munsch Early Readers · READING LEVEL 3 · READING BY MYSELF

50 BELOW ZERO

Story by **Robert Munsch**
Art by **Michael Martchenko**

Munsch Early Readers · READING LEVEL 3 · READING BY MYSELF

I HAVE TO GO!

Story by **Robert Munsch**
Art by **Michael Martchenko**

Munsch Early Readers · READING LEVEL 3 · READING BY MYSELF

MORTIMER

Story by **Robert Munsch**
Art by **Michael Martchenko**

Munsch Early Readers · READING LEVEL 3 · READING BY MYSELF

PIGS

Story by **Robert Munsch**
Art by **Michael Martchenko**

Munsch Early Readers · READING LEVEL 3 · READING BY MYSELF

The Paper Bag Princess

Story by **Robert Munsch**
Art by **Michael Martchenko**

All **Munsch Early Readers** are level 3, perfect for emergent readers ready for reading by themselves—because

READERS RULE!

Robert Munsch, author of such classics as *The Paper Bag Princess* and *Mortimer*, is one of North America's bestselling authors of children's books. His books have sold over 80 million copies worldwide. Born in Pennsylvania, he now lives in Ontario.

Michael Martchenko is the award-winning illustrator of the Classic Munsch series and many other beloved children's books. He was born north of Paris, France, and moved to Canada when he was seven.

© 2022 Bob Munsch Enterprises Ltd. (text)
© 2022 Michael Martchenko (illustrations)

Original publication:
© 1988 Bob Munsch Enterprises Ltd. (text)
© 1988 Michael Martchenko (illustrations)

Designed by Leor Boshi

Thank you to Abby Smart, B.Ed., B.A. (Honors), for her work on the educational exercises and for her expert review.

Annick Press Ltd.

All rights reserved. No part of this work covered by the copyrights hereon may be reproduced or used in any form or by any means—graphic, electronic, or mechanical—without the prior written permission of the publisher.

We acknowledge the support of the Canada Council for the Arts and the Ontario Arts Council, and the participation of the Government of Canada/la participation du gouvernement du Canada for our publishing activities.

Canada

ONTARIO ARTS COUNCIL
CONSEIL DES ARTS DE L'ONTARIO
an Ontario government agency
un organisme du gouvernement de l'Ontario

Library and Archives Canada Cataloguing in Publication

Title: Angela's airplane / story by Robert Munsch ; art by Michael Martchenko.
Names: Munsch, Robert N., 1945- author. | Martchenko, Michael, illustrator.
Description: Series statement: Munsch early readers | Reading level 3: reading with help.
Identifiers: Canadiana (print) 20220170916 | Canadiana (ebook) 20220170924 | ISBN 9781773216508 (hardcover) | ISBN 9781773216409 (softcover) | ISBN 9781773216638 (HTML) | ISBN 9781773216751 (PDF)
Subjects: LCSH: Readers (Primary) | LCGFT: Readers (Publications)
Classification: LCC PE1119.2 .M853 2022 | DDC j428.6/2—dc23

Published in the U.S.A. by Annick Press (U.S.) Ltd.
Distributed in Canada by University of Toronto Press.
Distributed in the U.S.A. by Publishers Group West.

Printed in China

annickpress.com
robertmunsch.com

Also available as an e-book. Please visit annickpress.com/ebooks for more details.